What? You haven't read the first Bad Dog book?
Go get it now!

Bad Dog and That Hollywood Hoohah

And look out for the next fur-raising adventure:

Bad Dog and the Curse of the President's Knee

BAD DOG

AND THOSE CRAZY MARTIANS

MARTIN CHATTERTON

SCHOLASTIC INC.

New York Toronto London Auckland Sydney
Mexico City New Delhi Hong Kong Buenos Aires

No part of this work may be reproduced, stored in a retrieval system, or transmitted in any form or by any means, electronic, mechanical, photocopying, recording, or otherwise, without written permission of the publisher. For information regarding permission, write to Scholastic Ltd., Commonwealth House, 1–19 New Oxford Street, London WC1A 1NU, United Kingdom.

ISBN 0-439-66159-5

12 11 10 9 8 7 6 5 4 3 2   5 6 7 8 9 10 / 0

Printed in the U.S.A.   40
First Scholastic printing, March 2005

CHAPTER 1

WHAT WE GOT HERE IS A FAILURE TO COMMUNICATE

Space travel ain't all it's cracked up to be.

In fact, I'd go so far as to say that it's a complete pain in the asteroids. Trust me, I know what I'm talking about. You're listening to the first dog on Mars. That's right: M-A-R-S. Big red dusty planet about fifty million miles from Earth. Now, a hundred million miles later, I'm back in my favorite cell with absolutely nothing to look forward to except bad food, cold floors, and a painful death. But, hey! Let's not get all sniffly about it.

Just kick back and let me tell you a shaggy Martian story.

It's a doozy.

For those of you who don't know me, the name's "Bad Dog." Not that I'm *bad,* you understand. I prefer to think of myself as misunderstood.

And where I am is Z-Block in the stinky old City Dog Pound. Z-Block is where all the unwanted dogs get dumped.

Fester is in charge of Z-Block and he just *loves* tormenting us pooches. The only thing he's got going for him from a doggy point of view is his amazingly ripe smell.

On my first stay in Z-Block, I was the next pooch in line to be snuffed when rich Hollywood agent Vince Gold spotted my raw talent and hunky good looks and swept me off to become The Most Famous Movie Star Dog in Hollywood (Hooray!).

But as soon as I exercised my dog-given right to hate cats, I fouled things up pretty good and ended up right back here.

I had everything: fame, looks, and money. All gone now.

Apart from the looks, obviously.

"I guess you movie stars must like things back here," said Fester when I arrived back. "Let me show you to your new luxury suite. I think you'll like our new facilities. Not. Now git movin'."

As far as I was concerned, Fester could paint himself pink and push peas down his pants, but on the block I didn't have any choice except to do as I was told. It was that or a one-way trip through the green door to Doggy Heaven.

I followed Fester to his new plaything. It was a small concrete bunker, with just one tiny window right at the top and a slot in the door. It was horrible.

"Welcome to The Hole," said Fester, a nasty grin pasted to his face. "How d'ya like it?"

"Like it?" I woofed. "I *love* it!" And, head in air, tail wagging, I trotted in. "Hold all my calls, Miss Murgatroyd. I don't want to be disturbed."

"You won't be so cocky after a coupla weeks in there," said Fester.

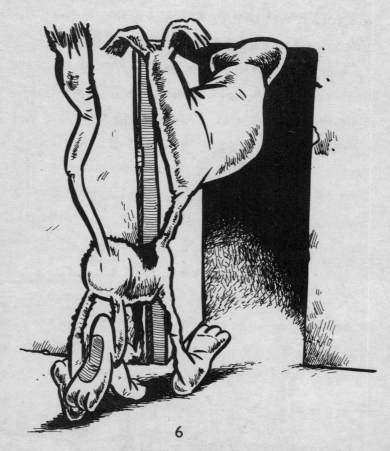

As soon as the steel door slammed shut I fell to the concrete floor weeping. Silently, of course, I didn't want that creep Fester to hear me.

"Quit that whinin'!" he shouted through the door.

Oops. I guess I can't have been as quiet as I thought. Memo to self: *Must practice stiff upper lip.*

As Fester's footsteps clicked off down the hall, I lay back and gazed up at the sky. Billions of twinkly little lights, winking away like fairy diamond dust on a velvet blanket, and I wished, I wished . . . I wished that I had a dirty big hunk of bloody steak right in front of me.

What do you expect? I'm a dog, not a poet.

If I'd known what was going to happen, perhaps I'd have looked a bit more closely at those stars.

CHAPTER 2

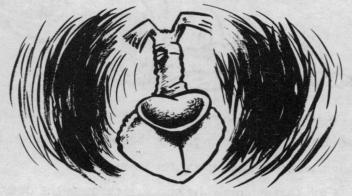

THE HOLE TRUTH

The days passed.

The weeks passed.

I picked up valuable tips from the pooches on the outside. The guys slipped me extra rations and whispered news through the walls to keep my spirits up. Although, to be honest, after life in Hollywood, I was quite enjoying The Hole. I concentrated on keeping my glorious physique in tip-top shape and practicing my sleeping technique.

One afternoon, in the middle of a good snooze, I was woken up by the sound of footsteps and the smell of Fester coming down the hall. There were more smells with him, more humans. My super-doggy sense of smell told me there were three of them.

Fester was nervous.

"This is the subject we've been told about?" said a deep, clipped voice.

"Er, yessir," said Fester.

"But isn't the usual amount of time a dog spends in solitary three days?" said another, weedy-sounding voice.

"That's right," said Fester.

"And this dog has been here, what, six weeks?" Deep Voice again.

"Er, yes," said Fester with a cough.

"Give me a canine status update, Johnson," said Deep Voice.

"Yessir. Right away, sir," said another voice. There was a rustling of paper.

"Our data tells us that this dog should be almost blind with forty percent muscle loss, thirty-five percent body-weight reduction, and missing most of his teeth. In short, we'd expect the subject to be very close to death after a period in solitary like this," said Johnson.

Hmm, I thought, *interesting*. Some sixth sense told me that this might be my chance to escape, and I dropped to the floor in a flash.

The door creaked open and light flooded in.

"123 . . . 124 . . . 125 . . ." I looked up from

pretending to do one-arm push-ups.

There was a sharp gasp from the circle of faces peering through the door.

"OK. Out!" yelled Fester.

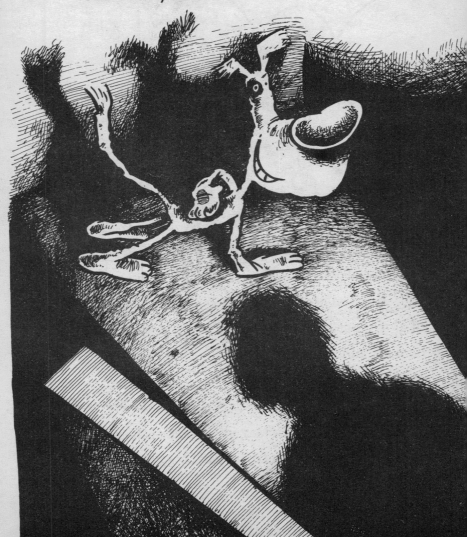

I bounced out
of The Hole,

threw in a couple of
handsprings for
good measure,

and stood in front
of a group of three
humans and Fester.

All the humans looked very official. Fester just
looked like a total twerp as usual.

The human nearest to me looked at me like he'd woken up on Christmas morning and I was a sock full of presents. He was thin and pale, dressed in a smart green uniform and holding a clipboard. "Oh, Commander Gouger!" he trilled. "I really think you've done it, sir! This one . . . well, he's perfect! You *are* clever! Good for you, Commander!"

"Can the kissing-up, Johnson," spat Deep Voice. "I can see for myself."

He stepped forward. The Commander was a tall, tanned man, with gray hair cut so short you could see his scalp through it and a chin you could land a helicopter on. He'd obviously stolen his eyes from some unfortunate shark. He was wearing a green uniform, but you could hardly see it under an avalanche of medals, gold braid, and ribbons.

He looked at me.

I looked at him.

"Hmm, he *is* in good condition, considering . . . used to pressure . . . confined spaces. You might be right, Johnson."

Johnson beamed.

The third man, or Weedy Voice, wasn't wearing a uniform. He was short and round, dressed in gray and wearing black spectacles with heavy rims.

"What's the background on this dog, Commander Gouger?" he said.

Gouger's large head swiveled towards him, and he quickly pasted a smile on his face.

"Well, Congressman McVitie, as you know, OSPEXA has been tracking multiple K9s around this DMZ 24/7. This canine profile interfaces with our assessment criteria to the hundredth percentile and I would advise that in the light of prior visual analysis, we act PDQ and obtain CEO authorization to activate egress under NatSec provision 73/6:2313131327788654X, effective ASAP."

McVitie must have looked puzzled because when Gouger spoke again, this time it was in English. "We've been looking for a dog like this for the past three months. I'm recommending that we take this one with us. How'd you like to come with us, Bad Dog? Woooooah! Erk! Boof! Yik! Shlip! Murf!"

You might be puzzled by that last bit. The "woooooah" stuff, I mean. That's because I'd just jumped into Commander Gouger's arms and was busy licking his face. He could take that as a yes.

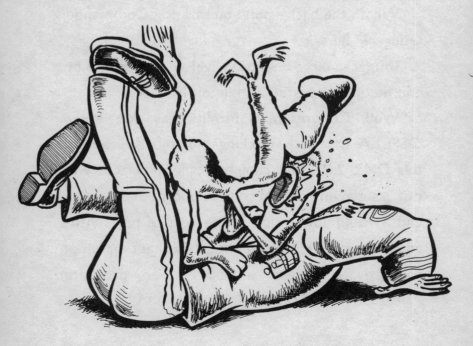

Gouger stood quickly and dropped me to the floor. He looked at me like I was something unpleasant he'd found on his shoe.

Johnson thrust a huge pile of paper at Fester, whose mouth was hanging open.

"Sign here, here, here, and here. And again here. This *is* a matter of national security and you are bound by paragraph 3456.9, subsection B, to say nothing about our visit to anyone, or anything, or to divulge Bad Dog's whereabouts. In fact, it's best if you forgot you ever knew a dog called Bad Dog." Johnson paused and looked up at Fester. "Failure to comply may result in, er, problems. Problems for you, that is. Have a nice day."

Fester spluttered and scrawled his name. I left, trotting alongside Commander Gouger and Congressman McVitie. I didn't really know where we were headed, but it had to be an improvement on this place. Right?

Chapter 3

There's Always a Catch, isn't There?

It was an improvement. A big one.

There was a catch, however. There's always a catch, isn't there? More on that later.

To be honest I was completely in the dark about just who these guys were and what they needed me for. All I knew was that they were an improvement on Fester and Z-Block.

Outside the pound stood an enormous green truck. A door slid open, we clambered aboard and headed out of town.

Inside, the van was packed with blinking computer screens, flashing lights, wires, and what seemed like dozens of people in white coats. There was an operating table in the middle. Two white-coats picked me up and stood me in the middle of it.

"I've already had my appendix out," I quipped. No one laughed.

Gouger and McVitie sat back in their seats, Johnson hovering somewhere just behind Gouger's shoulder.

"OK, people, let's get this operation moving!" said Gouger. He barked instructions and the people in the white coats started measuring me, taking photos, and running strange beeping scanner-type things over me. Keyboards clicked and printers clattered and I began to get a nagging doubt about my miraculous escape.

Now that I came to think about it, Gouger had said they were from something called OSPEXA.

"The dog matches the OSPEXA profile perfectly," said Gouger, leaning forward and looking at a computer readout.

"I hope you're right," said Congressman McVitie. "The Outer Space Exploration Agency has had quite enough time already to find a suitable specimen, Commander."

I jerked to attention. Outer space? Isn't that all that black stuff hanging up there in the sky? I began to get a small bad feeling about all this.

"With respect, Congressman, finding a canine like this for our experi — er, expedition is no easy task. We need a specimen who can cope with living in tiny spaces for long periods of time. A dog that can cope with pressure. A survivor. And I'm pleased to say I think we've got our dog," said Gouger.

Those bad feelings I was telling you about? They were getting bigger all the time. In fact, they had swollen to the size of a herd of greedy elephants on a weeklong cake binge.

Gouger looked at me as one of the white-coat boys rammed a thermometer in one of my most sensitive areas.

"Hey! That wasn't polite," I woofed. "My rear end is nobody else's business except mine and forty-two million other dogs'!" They didn't understand a word, of course.

"Pipe down, soldier!" snarled Gouger, directing a nasty look in my direction. I piped down.

He stood and slowly circled the table, his hands rammed into his pockets. He talked to McVitie but looked at me. Johnson drifted along behind him. "Most of the other specimens folded under pressure," said Gouger. "They couldn't cope with the training. Some of them practically dragged us back to the City Pound. But this one's different. It coped with The Hole.

It coped with being alone.

It has nothing to lose.

It's ugly, mangy, smelly, too old to be picked as a Christmas present, real stupid . . ."

I was starting to dislike Commander Gouger.

". . . more stupid than a cat, for example . . ."

This was going too far. As he came within range, I gave him a quick nip on the backside. See how he liked some rear-end pain.

"Ow!" he yelped. He turned and looked at me nastily, rubbing his bottom. "I don't know if you can understand me, mutt, but understand this: That wasn't smart. I'm Chief Field Commander of this project, and you need to remember that you're scheduled for extermination next month. Feel free to abort this mission at any time."

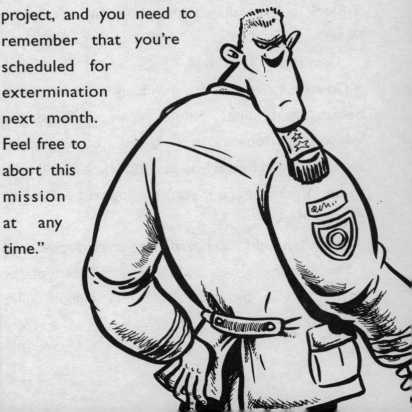

Ah. Yes. In the heat of the moment I had forgotten about that. Maybe Gouger had been right about the "stupid" bit.

"On the other hand, you *do* have the opportunity to serve your country and perhaps survive to become a hero. I'll leave it up to you." Gouger paused.

A hero? I can dig that, I thought.

"But bite me again and you'll be back on Z-Block quicker than you can say 'woof.' Got it, mutt?"

"I got it. Sir," I barked.

Gouger looked at me curiously for a moment before continuing. "Hmm. Now, settle down. We've got a long trip back to HQ. Training starts tomorrow and I want you in good shape. You'll *need* to be in good shape if you're going to be the first dog on Mars."

I wondered if I had heard Gouger correctly.

"Excuse me?" I gasped. "*Mars?* Big red planet floating up in the sky about fifty million miles from Earth?"

Gouger didn't say anything else, but at least I'd figured out exactly what that catch was.

I was going into space.

Chapter 4

Floating Monkey, Hidden Feline

I must have slept for quite some time, because when I woke it was daylight.

The truck was slowing. We came to a halt outside a huge white building with the biggest doors I had ever seen.

"We're here," said Gouger. "Let's get to work."

Once inside, we trotted down a long corridor for a couple of months until we came to Astronaut Experimentation Lab 4. An armed soldier stood guard outside. Johnson stepped forward and pressed the palm of his hand onto some hi-tech gizmo on the wall. The door slid back and I stepped inside. The room was a huge, white space, brightly lit and about as welcoming as the inside of a fridge.

"Make yourself at home, Bad Dog," said Gouger.

The door slid shut and I heard them walk away down the corridor.

Astronaut Experimentation Lab 4 was not empty. Or quiet.

Away to my left was a huge glass tank filled with dirt. The tank must have been nine feet tall and twenty feet long. There was a low sound of crunching coming from the tank. I trotted over for a closer look and saw that the case was packed with zillions of ants. It was an ant farm. A big one. I looked around the rest of the lab.

Wooden poles were placed across the room at different heights with thick ropes hanging down from them like hairy spaghetti. Some had tires attached.

On my right, on a long table, two white rats were trotting away on little treadmills. They looked for all the world like they were working out at the gym.

"We're just working out, old boy!" squeaked one of them. "Be with you in a minute. Got to keep the old pudge down, eh? Gouger's orders: We're carrying a little spare chub around the middle and it's got to come off before launch day! The name's Blenkinsop, Snowy Blenkinsop, formerly of Her Majesty's Fifth Royal Laboratory Research Division, Porton Down, Hampshire. And this lazy overweight rodent is Quentin Dimmock-Smythe. Everyone calls him Q."

Q winked at me and patted his belly, and they continued trotting around.

"Er, hi," I managed to reply just as a slice of pizza slapped onto the floor next to me. I looked up.

There was a monkey floating several yards above my head. It was wearing what looked like a space suit and eating pizza. I shook my head and tried to wake up.

"Do not adjust your set!" said the monkey, with an earsplitting cackle. "Normal service will be resumed as soon as we have this antigravity monkey suit under control! HAHA! HAHAHAHAHA!"

He clicked a button on the front of his suit, stuffed the rest of the pizza into his mouth, and drifted to the ground. As soon as his feet hit the deck he did three backflips, grabbed one of the wooden poles, and hung upside down.

"Dexter's the name, dog dude!" said the monkey, whipping off his helmet and sticking out a hand. "Lay some fur on me, man!"

I reached out a paw to shake but, in an instant, Dexter whipped his hand up to his nose and blew a fat raspberry at me.

"Me and you are going to have to sort a few things out," I said, giving the hairy comedian my best "look."

"Chill, babe," he said. "I'm just monkeying around. Lemme show you where you can flop."

My "room" was just a boxed-off area in one corner but it was warm, clean, and dry. And, of course, I wasn't facing certain death here. No, I was just going to be strapped into a dirty great big rocket and blasted off into outer space.

"This scene is, like, totally harmonious," said Dexter, peeling a banana he'd pulled from a huge bunch lying on a bench. "Dig it, bro': bone-soothin' bean bags, big-screen TV with cable and PlayStation, as much  food as you can munch. All you gotta do is keep Gouger happy. No problemo."

"'No problemo'?" I said. "What about the fact that pretty soon we'll be on our way to Mars?"

"Yeah, that is a bummer," said Dexter. "But the way I see it, my last gig was testing makeup remover by having it dropped in my eye. Bogus, or what? Three months of that kind of heinous behavior and Mars starts to look like a smooth ride on a soft wave."

Dexter had a point.

"Maybe things in OSPEXA Astronaut Experimentation Lab 4 aren't so bad," I said, taking a look around and thinking about all that hero stuff Gouger had spouted. I saw myself sitting in the back of a convertable as I got a ticker-tape reception from the adoring multitudes.

"That's the spirit!" said Snowy Blenkinsop, who had wandered over after his workout. "Accentuate the positive and all that. By the way, Gouger said there was someone else due in after you. This sounds like them now."

He pointed a pink nose at the door just as Gouger walked in, Johnson trailing in his wake. I trotted over, hoping the new recruit would be someone I could feel at home with — another canine perhaps, or, failing that, a chameleon, crocodile, cormorant, cod, or coyote.

Anything except a cat.

After all, I *was* going to be sharing digs with this lot for a while.

"This is Tiddles, everyone," said the Gouge, nodding at the creature curled up in his arms.

It was a cat.

Chapter 5

The Ant Farm Incident

Did I mention my problem with cats? No?

Well, let me put the record straight.

I hate cats. I know you're going to say, "Well, of course you hate cats, you fool, you're a *dog*. You're *supposed* to hate cats."

This is true, but the way I hate cats goes way beyond all that normal dog/cat thing. I *really* hate 'em.

I stared at the repulsive thing. I'd just spent six

weeks in solitary because of cats! And now here was another that I was expected to cozy up to on a jolly jaunt to Mars.

Gouger wasn't looking quite as robot-like as usual. He was cuddling the repulsive cat-thing and looking down at it adoringly.

"Is ickle Tiddles all tired out then?" he said, tickling the vile beast under its chin and smiling at it in a completely vom-making way. The cat purred loudly and stared at us in that sly, superior way that makes you think it knows something you don't. Gouger seemed to have completely lost his marbles. "Will Daddy get oo a lickle bowl of milky-wilky den?" he gushed.

I nearly passed out on the spot from sheer disgust and embarrassment.

Snowy and Q weren't looking too thrilled at the prospect of life with Tiddles, either. Especially as the beast was eyeing them and licking his horrible little cat lips.

Dexter had floated off and was hovering somewhere up near the ceiling.

Tiddles looked at me. "Dog-breath," he said.

"Furball," I shot back, sharp as a razor.

"Bone-eating tail-sniffer," said Tiddles.

"Flea-infested feline." Me again.

I didn't wait for the comeback.

The time for witty banter was over — I sprang into action. As the most intelligent, and best-looking, of the Mars Team, I felt that I acted for everyone when I leaped at Tiddles, fangs bared, and tried to separate his head from his neck.

Tiddles must have been expecting my attack. As I lunged forward he sneakily jumped onto Gouger's head, sinking his claws into the commander's scalp and spitting at me. Tiddles was spitting, not Gouger.

"NNNnnmmNNNAAAGGGHHHNNNNN!!" shrieked Gouger, spinning around. I could barely hear his pitiful screams, as I was too busy jumping up, barking and snarling at the devil beast clamped to his noggin.

"Come on, cat! Let's get it on, you feline freak!" I yapped.

Tiddles made a break for it and sprang to the top of the glass tank containing the ant farm. As soon as he got there he turned rigid with fear. It's a cat thing. You know what they're like. Always getting stuck up trees and having to be rescued. Pathetic.

Gouger fell to his knees moaning while Johnson dabbed at his head with a hankie.

It was a standoff. The cat stood on the rim of the glass tank above me and I bounced around like a hairy yo-yo, unable to get high enough to do any serious cat-whupping.

Suddenly Gouger scrambled to his feet, his face red, sweaty, and furious. "You, I'll deal with later!" he snapped at me. He grabbed a chair and, helped by Johnson, gingerly climbed up onto the edge of the ant tank where Tiddles stood, frozen to the spot.

Nervously, Gouger started inching along the top of the tank towards the cat. "Come on, precious," he whispered. "Come to Daddy."

As he got closer he reached out and carefully took hold of Tiddles. Tiddles gave me a real smug look and made a suggestion about my parents that would have made a seafaring Rottweiler blush.

It was too much for a red-blooded, cat-chasin' hound like me to take. Summoning up all my strength I made an almighty leap for Tiddles.

A moment later I was wrapped around Gouger's trouser leg.

"Let go, you nasty mutt!" he snarled, kicking out at me. "That's a direct order!"

Never let it be said that I would disobey a direct order from a superior officer. Besides, he was kicking me in the jaw with his size 13s.

I let go.

Gouger obviously hadn't expected me to, because he started to wobble. Frantically flapping his arms to keep his balance, he stood for a breathless moment on the edge of the glass tank.

It was no use. With a cry, Gouger and Tiddles toppled back, falling into the soft mulchy soil of the ant farm, facedown.

"Commander!" squealed Johnson. He yelled for help into a little intercom on the wall, then scampered around looking for a ladder to help Gouger out.

Gouger was stuck. His legs waved around in the air and a strange, muffled, girlish scream came from his half-submerged mouth as millions of ants started to run up his pant legs. They were swarming all over him, but I guessed it was the ants-in-the-pants that were producing the screams. Tiddles was coughing and spluttering as he, too, disappeared under a swarming mass of ants.

Snowy and Q were rolling around on the floor laughing their tails off. Ditto Dexter, but thanks to the antigravity suit, he was rolling around on the ceiling.

"Oops," I barked. "Sorry!" (I wasn't sorry, of course. Not even a little bit. In fact, I settled back to watch the show.)

Two soldiers burst in. Together with Johnson, they scooped Gouger and Tiddles out. Gouger's head, and much of the rest of him, was totally covered in a seething black mass of ants. Only the tail sticking out identified Tiddles as a cat.

Gouger started doing a freaky dance, leaping up and down and slapping himself all over while spitting out gobfuls of wet ants and yodeling at the same time.

Tiddles was bouncing around the room dislodging clumps of ants every time he collided with something.

"Yeeerahhhggghhhhhhhhoooooooooooooahahhah hahnnnnenenenenenenenaaaHHHNNNGAH!" screamed Gouger as he windmilled past me, trailing a thick cloud of ants behind him.

He dug frantically at his underwear, shaking his head wildly from side to side, legs flailing out as if electric shocks were being applied to his knees. He ripped off most of his clothing in a few seconds and frantically scooped out more handfuls of ants from his undies. Then he pointed at me, his breath coming out in short ragged bursts.

"FRSHOOFT FTHAT SHDOG!!" he screamed. The two soldiers looked baffled. Gouger spat out a mouthful of ants. "Shoot that dog!" he yelled at them. "Shoot the darn dog! NOW!!!"

They hesitated and looked at each other, but (and here was the worrisome part) they then raised their guns and looked at me.

"GO ON! YOU IDIOTS!!! *SHOOT HIM!*" screamed Gouger, just as the door opened and Congressman McVitie and a brisk-looking, gray-haired woman in a military uniform stepped into the room. She had a face like a bulldog chewing a wasp.

"It's The Controller!" whispered Snowy. "The Big Cheese!"

"Commander Gouger," said the woman. "Care to let me know what's going on here?"

"The dog, he — I — we should — er, that is —" spluttered Gouger. "HE STARTED IT!"

"Get yourself cleaned up and back on track, Commander. This project is behind schedule already without you playing the fool."

Gouger opened his mouth to explain, but The Controller held up her hand and he fell silent.

"And take the cat with you."

"Of course, Controller," he said, his voice quivering with rage.

Gouger picked up Tiddles. He shot me a laser look.

"Zero six hundred hours tomorrow!" he spat. "*You* can meet Marge."

He spun around, saluted The Controller, and with as much dignity as he could muster, stalked out of the room in his boxer shorts. Johnson followed behind.

The Controller looked at me, Snowy, Q, and Dexter. "As you were," she said, turning and marching briskly away, McVitie whispering furiously in her ear.

"Phew!" I said. "I thought Gouger was going to get me back with something a lot worse than meeting Marge, whoever she is."

Snowy, Q, and Dexter looked at one another. Then they looked at me. From their faces I figured that meeting Marge might not be quite the stroll in the park I was counting on.

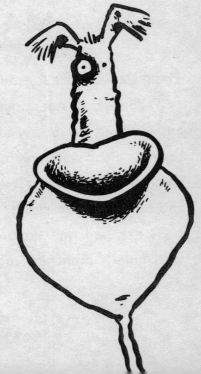

CHAPTER 6

MARGE

The guys wouldn't say much about Marge.

"Perhaps best not to eat too much, old boy," said Snowy. Then he muttered something about having to look into "watching my back." He wouldn't say any more but he and Q went back to their bunker and seemed to be discussing something.

Dexter had quit floating and contented himself with quietly munching most of the ants spilled by

Gouger and Tiddles. He sat on the floor picking up the ants one by one and apologizing to them as he popped them in his mouth. "Sorry, little insect dude. Sorry, man. Sorry."

In the morning, Gouger arrived in a fresh uniform accompanied by Johnson and McVitie. Tiddles sat in a comfy-looking basket on the backseat of their electric cart. Gouger's face was covered in tiny red bite marks, and his right eye was twitching ever so slightly.

He fixed me with a laser-beam stare. "Day One," he said. "Let's see if we made the right decision."

That didn't sound good.

"Right. Let's go. Don't want to keep Marge waiting, do we?" he said, a glassy smile pasted onto his face.

Out of the corner of my eye, and out of sight of the humans, I noticed Snowy and Q slip onto the back of the golf cart and hunker down. I winked at Dexter, who gave me the thumbs-up. I trotted through the door, tail held high, and hopped onto the cart, looking much more confident than I felt.

We drove along a maze of corridors to an elevator that dropped us a few floors underground. Then along another white-walled corridor. A loud electronic hum filled the air and the floor gently vibrated, as if a very large monster were snoring somewhere close. We stopped outside a metal door and everyone hopped down from the cart. I couldn't see Snowy or Q anywhere.

Gouger smiled unpleasantly at me.

"Meet Marge," he said, swinging open the door. "Marge" sat, squat, heavy, and threatening, in the center of a huge, circular, windowless room. She was huge — ten thousand tons of steel and cable pinned down by a circular metal floor brace.

Two arms made from steel beams stuck out from either side of the brace. At the end of one arm was a massive weight. On the end of the other was a strange-looking box about the size of an airplane cockpit.

"This is the Military Acceleration Rotary Gyroscope Edition 22," said Gouger to Congressman McVitie.
"'Marge' for short."

I still didn't see where I fit into the picture. Maybe this wasn't going to be so bad, after all. I began to relax. Marge was big, sure, but she didn't seem too bad on first glimpse.

"Marge is where we test how our astronauts deal with a rocket leaving Earth's atmosphere," Gouger hissed, giving me a sideways glance.

"The dog will be placed in the cockpit and Marge will spin him around at one thousand five hundred miles an hour, imitating the exact effects of being strapped in a rocket with five million gallons of rocket fuel igniting just below your seat. It's kind of like sitting in a giant washing machine set on 'spin'."

With a sinking heart I saw where I fell into all this.

Oh, goody. Sounds like fun.

"What about the dog?" said McVitie. "Is this dangerous?"

"Oh, yes," said Gouger, eyeing me. "But then we *can* always find another dog, can't we?"

Behind me, Tiddles snickered.

Two of the white-coats strapped me in and clipped little wires all over me before disappearing through a small door. I could see everyone watching me on a monitor. I could also see them on a small video screen straight in front of me.

Gouger, with Tiddles cradled in one arm, was at the controls. I watched as he pressed a key on the computer. Instantly, Marge started to hum and the cockpit began to turn. At first, Marge turned very slowly and it was quite pleasant. I kept glimpsing Gouger as we whizzed past. Gradually the speed increased and pretty soon I couldn't see Gouger, or the control room, unless I looked at the video screen.

I began to wish I'd taken Snowy's advice. Last night's anchovy, sausage, chili, and pineapple pizza began to take on a life of its own deep in the bowels of my bowels.

Marge cranked up a gear and my face began to wobble uncontrollably as what felt like a huge hand pushed me back into the seat, hard. My eyes bulged, my teeth vibrated like a bag of nails in a food blender, and I was whacked in the eye by something flapping like a wet flag in a high wind. It was my tongue.

As if that weren't enough, there was a large wrestler sitting on my chest, or at least that's exactly what it felt like.

Round and round and round and round we went.

Up on the screen I could see Gouger, bent over the computer controls. On the intercom I could hear some of the white-coats getting excited.

"Commander, the subject is approaching G-Force 15! WARNING! *Potential exploding dog scenario warning!*"

I didn't like the sound of the exploding dog scenario one little bit, but as all my efforts were concentrated on stopping my nose from migrating back through my eyelids, I didn't have time to be worried.

On-screen, Gouger just cackled uncontrollably at the white-coats. "More!" he yelled, stabbing his fingers at the keyboard. "HAHAHAHAHAHAHA HAHAHAHAHAHA!!!! MORE! MORE! MORE!"

Congressman McVitie was fiddling with his clipboard. "Er, is this normal, Commander?" he asked.

"OH, YES!" bellowed Gouger. "EVERYTHING IS PERFECTLY NORMAL!"

By now Marge was making a horrible, loud, high-pitched whining sound.

No, when I checked again, that was me. My eyes started to mist over. I couldn't close them because the lids were being slowly peeled back, making me goggle like a demented fish. My lips were flapping back around, south of my ears somewhere.

The wrestler sitting on my chest had been joined by a couple of baby hippos. The three of them had obviously hit it off because they were all dancing the marimba in lead boots.

"*G-Force 20 exceeded!!!*" screamed a white-coat.

Just before my vision stopped completely I caught a glimpse of Snowy Blenkinsop on the video screen.

I prepared to explode all over the cockpit.

I tried to scream but nothing came out.

Suddenly Marge made a weird popping sound. She crackled and fizzed a bit, and we began to slow down. For a moment I thought this was it, that I was on my way to Doggy Heaven . . . to the big lamppost in the sky.

But it turned out I wasn't quite dead yet. With a sound like a giant jet engine being switched off we gradually came to a halt. A thin wisp of smoke rose up from somewhere in Marge's innards.

My face had been rearranged. I looked like someone had inserted a vacuum cleaner in my head and switched it to "blow."

As my vision came back I could see Gouger hopping about and yelling. Then I spotted Snowy and Q being chased around the control room by the white-coats.

From what I could pick up on the monitor, it seemed that Snowy and Q had eaten their way through the power cable and saved me from death at the hands of Marge.

Hooray! I've always liked rats.

I was unstrapped from Marge and dumped in the golf cart. Walking was out of the question as my legs had been replaced by sacks of jelly. By now Snowy and Q had been nabbed and put in a small cage in the back of the cart.

"Thanks, fellas," I managed to cough.

"Don't mention it, Bad Dog," said Snowy. "Couldn't stand back and see a fellow astronaut splattered all over the place, could we?"

Then Gouger appeared, steam coming out of his ears. McVitie stood in the background taking notes.

"You might think you've put one over on me this time, you *vermin*," Gouger hissed. "But training ain't over. Let's see how you cope with the rest."

I leaned forward and carefully barfed last night's anchovy and pineapple pizza all over Gouger's shiny black shoes. I just caught a glimpse of Gouger's face reddening as everything went black, and I gratefully passed out.

CHAPTER 7

We Have a Go Situation

When I opened my eyes I was floating around about twenty feet off the floor. Snowy, Q, and Dexter were bobbing around in midair, too.

"Welcome back, floaty dog dude!" said Dexter. "How're you feelin'?"

"A little light-headed, to be honest," I quipped. Pretty sharp, considering how bad I felt. I looked down. "So. We're weightless," I said, proving how quick my powers of observation were.

I checked out the antigravity suit I was wearing. Pretty cool threads, all things considered.

"We've been up here for hours," said Snowy. "Gouger's only supposed to keep us up here for fifteen minutes at a time. He's seeing if he can push us over the edge."

Gouger was below us, standing over to one side, holding Tiddles as usual. The cat obviously didn't need any training. Gouger kept glancing up at me. Maybe he was anxious about another unexpected delivery of used pizza.

Congressman McVitie stood behind him, taking more notes and tutting. Johnson was twittering around Gouger.

Gouger seemed happy to let us float around until Christmas, but eventually McVitie lost his patience and persuaded Gouger to get on with the next part of our training.

This involved us finding objects in a big dark room. Gouger and McVitie watched us, using infrared night vision goggles. There were obstacles everywhere, but with my nose, Dexter's acrobatic ability, and the rats' skill with mazes, we soon found everything.

"This is kinda fun," said Dexter. "But what's the point of it all?"

"I have no idea, Dex," I replied. "But I think it's about time we found out." I sloped over to where Gouger and McVitie were standing, pretended to be sniffing something interesting in a corner, and cocked an ear to their chatter. It was easy to hear what they were saying because they were arguing, and besides, they didn't take the slightest notice of me. I'm just a dog, after all.

I found out some very interesting stuff:

1) We were heading to Mars for one reason: to find alien life (GULP!) and bring some of it back home.

2) They needed us to find the aliens because we were better at finding stuff than humans. Well, that figures.

3) Gouger wanted to leave the ants behind. Understandable.

4) All the animals could be left behind on Mars if need be. That bit I didn't like the sound of.

5) McVitie was coming with us to keep an eye on things.

I reported back to the guys and we thought about escape. For about five seconds.

"This place is locked up tighter than a banker's wallet," said Dexter.

"Besides," said Snowy. "Where we are is still better than where we were."

Good point, well put. We decided to stay and see this thing through. After all, I did have that ticker-tape parade to look forward to.

The next morning we were taken to see the rocket.

"There she is, Congressman," said Gouger, pointing out the eight-hundred-foot-high rocket in front of us, in case no one had noticed it. "Ark 2. The biggest rocket ever constructed. Isn't she lovely?"

"Er, it's big, isn't it?" said McVitie, fingering his glasses. I think he was starting to regret hitching a ride.

"Lemme get this right," I said. "Ark 2 is a ginormous tube filled with highly explosive rocket fuel. And we get strapped to the top of it while someone lights the fuse? Can anyone tell me what's wrong with this picture?"

No one was listening. Typical.

We passed below the massive engine cowlings and took the elevator to the top. From the ground the actual spaceship part of the rocket looked tiny, but close-up it was actually fairly large. The main control room was right at the front, pointing straight up at the sky. Behind the main control room were a gazillion storage bays, hallways, and rooms full of electronic stuff beeping away like crazy. All over the place white-coats fiddled around, adjusting things. Radio instructions crackled.

All of us animals looked nervously at one another.

They hadn't been kidding.

We were going to Mars.

CHAPTER 8

PUT THE PEDAL TO THE METAL

I lay back in my seat on board Ark 2, strapped up tighter than an Egyptian mummy, and looked out of the window. I'd requested an aisle seat but Mission Control gave me the window. Arf! Arf!

Launch day. Two minutes to go.

Gouger, with Tiddles strapped in right next to him, was in hog heaven, pushing little buttons and talking very seriously into his microphone. "That's an affirmative *crackle* Control *hiss*. We are prepped and *crackle* A-OK to proceed to prelim *hiss* ignition procedure."

He was loving it. I, on the other hand, wasn't quite so positive about this whole takeoff thing, but I was pleased to see I wasn't the only lily-livered coward on board. Congressman McVitie looked as though he was having second, third, and fourth thoughts about coming with us.

Johnson looked calm enough but it was hard to tell; that little reptile always looked a bit white and clammy.

I looked over to where Snowy and Q sat locked into their own little rat space outfits. They were probably just as nervous as anyone, but their British stiff upper lips were firmly in place. Dexter, in complete chill mode, had a pair of headphones on and was busy imitating Gouger.

"Like, yeah, we are *crackle* totally ripped to the max for cranking this baby upside and *hiss* putting the pedal to the metal, Control dudes. Heh heh heh!"

It needed work.

Tiddles was asleep next to Gouger. Typical cat: too stupid to be scared.

The ants were not going to Mars after all. Gouger had managed to convince Mission Control they weren't needed.

On the intercom the electric voice of The Controller cut across us.

"ENTERING FINAL IGNITION PHASE. 10-9-8-7 –"

This was it. As the preignition burners ignited the whole rocket started to shudder and whine.

"6-5-4 –"

The main rocket fuel burner ignited and Ark 2 bucked violently against the control tower. Harsh metal clangs and bangs came from outside as the gantry holding us up was released.

"3-2-1. We have final ignition, ARK 2. You are on your way."

With an enormous WHUMP! we slowly began to nose upwards. The four thirty-yard boosters kicked in and we were slammed back hard into our seats as the rocket exploded from the tower.

"WHAAAAAAAAAAAAAAAAAOOOOOO OOOOOOOOOOOOOOOOOOO!!!!!!" said someone, everyone, me.

Nothing in training, not even my meeting with Marge, had prepared me for the speed we were traveling. Everything on board the ship, and on board me, was shaking like a loose jackhammer. Outside, everything grew darker. The noise and shaking became almost unbearable and then — POP! — we were floating silently in inky-black space. The straps holding us into our seats automatically released and magically we were floating, too. No sooner were we weightless than Gouger snapped a switch and the anti-weightless equipment kicked in and we dropped back down to the deck of the Ark.

"Mission Control calling Ark 2. Confirm *crackle* that you have left Earth's orbit *hiss*."

"Affirmative, Control *crackle*," said Gouger. "I have command."

I swear his jaw grew an extra inch or two as he puffed his chest out. He knew the onboard cameras were relaying everything back to the folks back home. There was going to be only one hero on this trip if he had anything to do with it.

We settled into life on board. It was going to take us three weeks to get there and nothing much happened except that Gouger made us do more experiments. I had to try and find objects by sniffing them out; Dexter was given stuff to juggle and swing on. Snowy and Q were given a treadmill. "I knew it!" spat Snowy, disgusted. "Always trot out the treadmill for the rodents!"

Tiddles's experiments seemed to consist of scarfing down as many tuna treats as Gouger could stuff into his furry trap. Tiddles washed down the treats with dishes of cream from the huge supply of the stuff Gouger had brought aboard for his ickle precious baby.

Most of the time we slept. And, despite being in *space* on an actual *spaceship* . . . it was all pretty boring really. So let's fast-forward, *frrrriiiiibbbbllllllluppppppp*, to us actually reaching the red planet.

I snapped out of my daydream and, through the window of the Ark's explorer pod, watched the surface of Mars drift closer. We had left Ark 2 in the hands of Johnson and Tiddles and set off down to Mars to collect some Martian rocks.

Gouger aimed the Pod towards a flat-topped hill we could see to our left. Beyond the hill lay a range of spiky red mountains. The sky was yellow and red, fading to black.

As we touched down on Mars everyone was very quiet. The hatch on the Pod slid open, and a ramp dropped to the floor, stirring up a cloud.

We climbed into the SEV, the Surface Exploration Vehicle, and rolled down the ramp. Mars was covered in a layer of dust, sand, and rocks but the giant wheels of the SEV rode along easily. After a few yards we stopped and Gouger unrolled a flag.

This was his big moment.

He stood up and began to step from the vehicle. He was speaking in a funny, slow, deep voice into the camera strapped to the front of the SEV. "On behalf of all the peoples of Earth, I, Commander Oswald Taylor Miflin Gouger the Third, say simply this: Yarrrroooooh!"

This probably wasn't what he meant to say, but just as he stepped from the car I noticed something move off to our left behind some rocks. It moved quickly, but there was something about it I didn't like. I barked and Gouger, startled, missed his footing and fell headfirst out of the SEV. I jumped down onto him to get a better view of whatever was out there, barking loudly.

"Get off me, you idiot dog!" he yelled, scrambling around. He got up and jabbed the flag angrily into the dirt. "What are you three laughing at?" he snarled, stepping back into the SEV.

This last was directed at Dexter, Snowy, and Q, who were rolling around hysterically on the backseat of the SEV. They stopped laughing. Mostly.

"Let's get on with it, shall we, Commander?" said McVitie. "I don't want to waste time bickering. This mission is costing the taxpayer 8.2 million dollars a minute. What's he making all that racket about?"

That racket was me. I *had* seen something, and now I was making like a dog and barking my head off. And, now that I was closer to the ground I could smell . . . something odd.

Something familiar.

Something I didn't like.

If I didn't know we were on Mars and Tiddles was back on Ark 2, I could swear I caught a distinct whiff of . . . *cat*.

"Get back in this vehicle or I'll leave you right here!" snapped Gouger.

"But," I barked, "I saw something move! And I can smell something, too. We gotta go see what it is!"

"Right on, dude!" chimed in Dexter. "Dog says he smelled somethin', you'd better believe it! Let's roll!"

"Got to be worth taking a squint at surely, old boy?" said Snowy, looking at Gouger as though he could understand rat-speak.

"Can it!" shouted Gouger. "Or you'll all be left here along with the dog! Now get back in the vehicle, soldier!"

That shut all of us up. I mean Mars looked OK for a windswept, dusty dump, but you wouldn't want to spend longer than, say, two minutes out here. With one last look around I jumped back on board and we went off to collect some rocks. As we pulled away I thought I heard something from behind the rocks where the smell was. I couldn't be certain but it sounded to me like laughter. I just hoped that we weren't going to be the punch line.

CHAPTER 9

LIFE ON MARS

Safely back aboard the Pod with as fine a collection of rocks as anyone could wish for, I got together with the guys and we discussed what to do.

"There's something down there," I said.

"That's for sure," said Dexter. "Question is, do we really want to check out exactly what sort of something it is?"

"Dexter may have a point," chipped in Snowy. Q nodded in agreement.

"I'm not too anxious to help Gouger," I said. "But one thing's certain: If we do find something down there, there's no way we'll have to go back to where we came from. We'd be famous. We'd be on Easy Street."

That got their attention.

"I think that we should investigate The Mystery of the Smelly Martians the next chance we get," I added. "What have we got to lose?"

There was general agreement (He'd just been promoted from Major Agreement . . . Arf! Arf!) and we settled down for our first night on Mars.

I didn't get a lot of sleep. I was busy chasing a million chocolate rabbits across an emerald pasture when one of them started shouting my name.

"Bad Dog! Bad Dog! Wake up!"

I opened my eyes. Disappointingly, it wasn't the chocolate rabbit, it was Dexter. "Multo scary happenings, dude!" he whispered.

"There's something moving around outside."

"Maybe it's just Gouger fixing something," I replied.

"Yeah, probably he's changing a tire. I think we ran over a nail back there," said Dexter, narrowing his eyes. "This is some freaky alien-type noise thing, dude! Get your tail in gear. We gotta go see."

The Pod lay silent as we trotted to a window. Snowy and Q were already pressing their snouts against the glass.

"Can't see a blessed thing out there," said Snowy as we approached.

"Listen," whispered Dexter.

"I can't hear anyth —" I started to say, when I heard it. Something was on the roof of the Pod. We all looked towards the ceiling as whatever was out there moved above us. A tapping, scratching sound came from the metal.

"Claws!" hissed Dexter. "That sounds like claws."

He was right and I shivered. Whatever was out there sounded huge.

Huge and with claws.

I was about to speak when there was an incredible screaming howl from above. We clamped paws to ears and winced in pain. The sound rose and fell in pitch and was like . . . *like a crying baby.*

"What is *that?*" yelped Dexter.

"I think I've heard that sound before," I replied. "It's —"

Before I had a chance to tell the guys, the door flew open and Gouger and McVitie stormed in.

"What! What, who? Whaaa?" Gouger had just woken up and was getting his bearings. "Which one of you is making that racket?" he bellowed.

I pointed to the ceiling. Gouger and McVitie looked up, and their mouths fell open as they realized the noise was coming from outside the Pod.

And then, as suddenly as it had started, the sound stopped. The silence was like a cool bath. We all breathed a long sigh and then rushed to the window.

Nothing.

Outside was Mars and plenty of it. But no mysterious creatures. No racing shadows. Nothing.

Gouger began to recover and gripped McVitie by his pajamas. "You know what this means, don't you?" he yelled. "We've found life on Mars!"

"I-I-I-I think, th-that perhaps we ought to, er, that is, um, ah . . . leave," stuttered the congressman.

"LEAVE?" yelled Gouger. "Do you realize how important this could be? At first light we're going after that thing!"

He left the room, his eyes alight with thoughts of fame. McVitie trotted after him looking distinctly greenish.

We all looked at each other after they had left.

"Phew!" said Dexter. "I hope that dude knows what he's doing."

Snowy looked at me. "BD, old boy, before Gouger burst in, you said that you'd heard that sound before. What did you mean?"

I looked at them. "I *have* heard the sound before. You all have. It's singing."

"Singing!" said Snowy. "I've never heard anything sing like that!"

"Oh, you have," I said. "There's only one animal that sings like that."

They all looked at me.

"That was a cat," I said. "A big one."

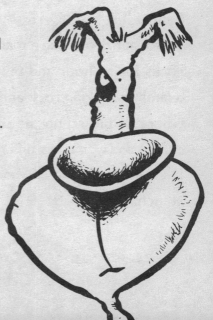

CHAPTER 10

BONGO FURY

The next morning we set out in the SEV on an alien hunt.

Gouger drove like a maniac. We bounced over the rocks for an hour and saw nothing. Then we passed a familiar-looking rock and I knew we were close to where I'd picked up the scent yesterday.

And today was no different. My nostrils twitched, I leaped from the SEV and raced after the feline stench.

Behind me I was dimly aware of Gouger yelling stuff in my direction as I scampered across the dusty ground towards the rocks and *that* smell, all my cowardly thoughts gone now that I knew we were dealing with a cat.

"Wait up!" Gouger's voice crackled through my earpiece.

Dexter, Snowy, and Q jumped ship, too, and started running after me.

"We're right behind you, dude!" yelled Dexter through the headset.

I picked up the scent again and legged it around the ragged rocks.

Gouger gave up trying to stop us, and the SEV started up in our direction.

On the other side of the rocks was a rocky canyon. Steep walls rose up on either side of me, and it was much darker here than out on the flat-topped hill. As I followed the scent, the walls closed as the canyon narrowed. I came to a halt in a sort of cave. In the darkness I noticed some odd-shaped white objects under my paw. I sniffed at one of them.

A bone. Whoo-hoo! I quickly buried it in the dirt. You never know when a good bone will come in handy.

Up ahead I could hear sly little rustling movements. There were one or two little squeaking noises, too. Suddenly I was aware that I was alone, on a strange planet, in a dark cave with spooky noises coming out of it. And now that I had time to think about it, whose bones had I just stepped on?

So I did what any self-respecting dog would do: I stopped, and started barking in a very chesty manner without actually going any farther into the  cave. Then I remembered the huge singing thing (with claws) from last night and shut up. Quickly.

Dexter loped up with Snowy and Q on his shoulders. "What's happenin', dude?" he said. "You made like a banana and split. Did you get a call on the old nose phone?"

"Listen," I whispered, although I don't know why I was whispering after the racket I'd been making.

The four of us stood, breathing softly. From inside the cave came a soft, rhythmic, rumbling sound. It sounded familiar, but I couldn't quite place it.

"You know," said Q, "I've heard that sound somewhere very recently."

"Me, too," I replied.

Over the top of this background rhythm was something else. Music. Strange plinky-plonky sort of music.

Behind us the SEV was rumbling towards the cave, and gradually the headlights began to cast some light into the darkness. Peering ahead, I noticed hundreds of bright green circles bobbing slowly about.

"I know what they are," squeaked Snowy. "They're *eyes*!"

"And that sound," shouted Q. "It's *purring*!"

I had a very bad feeling about this.

The SEV headlights bounced over some rocks, and suddenly the cave was flooded with light.

"CATS!" I screamed.

And there they were. Hundreds of the things sitting all over the cave, their horrid little green eyes reflecting back the beams from the SEV.

My first instinct was to go on the attack and do some serious cat-whuppin'.

However, after a closer look, I could see that there were far too many of them, even for a tail-kickin' pooch like me. There were cats sitting on every inch of the cave and they seemed to stretch back as far as we could see. I nearly gagged.

One more thing: The cats were gently bobbing their heads up and down, and playing an assortment of odd-shaped musical instruments.

One near the front was singing. I think.

"Feeblydoo a-shim bam boogy!
Diddlyscam fer reep pan oogy!
Diddle-um, diddle-um, diddle-um boof!"

Behind us Gouger and McVitie had gotten down from the SEV and were staring at the Martian cats.

"Unbelievable!" said Gouger.

"Remarkable!" said McVitie. "This must have been what was making that racket on the Pod last night."

"Dig that galactic jazz vibe, man!" said Dexter, snapping his fingers in time to the beat. "Like crazy, daddy-o!"

Now that I looked closer I could see that the Martian cats were different from Earth cats. They were different sizes for a start, the biggest of them the size of a small elephant, and the smallest no bigger than Snowy and Q. They were also covered in strange markings and had wire-like antennae popping out from the tops of their heads.

Oh, and one other small difference: Most of them were wearing sunglasses.

One of them, fat, sleek, and bright yellow, put down the bongo drums it had been lightly thumping, slid softly down from a small ledge, and moved towards us.

"Shmabble dip oooly fribbler splish futnip," it said, looking at us and smiling. "Berlong croffdip."

Er, right. This was going to take some work.

Gouger produced a small device from a pocket of his suit and held it up to his mouth.

"Let's see if this little gizmo can help. It's a state-of-the-art intergalactic universal translator."

He pressed a switch and spoke into the device. "Greetings. We come in peace."

From the machine came an electronic voice. "Freeble dipshot urk noof bibble tooog."

The Martian cat obviously understood what Gouger had said, because it smiled and coiled itself around his legs.

"Bing bang bong eeplyboffy yay pingpong! Kaboom, diffler stiffler shboom neep deep fatong berfe di funnelty ping poom!"

We waited as the translation device absorbed all this. It crackled and then out came the first words from the Martian.

That was it? "Miaow"? Fifty million miles and all they can say is "miaow"? I knew that cats were dumb, even Martian ones, but surely they could come up with something better than that?

But Gouger was delighted, the cat-lovin' dipstick. "Aaah!" he gushed, tickling the top of the Martian cat's head. "They're just regular pussycats like back home!"

With the help of the translator Gouger asked the Martian cat if he/she/it would like to come with us back to Earth.

When the rest of the cats heard this they started laughing. The sort of laugh a tribe of cannibals might make if you invited them for some lunch.

"I don't like the sound of that," whispered Snowy in my ear.

"Me, neither," I replied.

The cat nodded at Gouger and I knew, just *knew*, that the guy was making a serious misjudgment. I tried to tell him but he was having none of it.

"Quit that yapping. We've done what we came here to do: find alien life. We're going back to the Ark. Mission accomplished. Case closed."

I started to tell him again but he cut me off. "Of course you are welcome to stay here," he said, doing that laser-eye thing again.

"Let's go!" I said quickly. "We can't keep our guest waiting, can we?" Pathetic, I know, but I did *not* want to be stuck on this planet with all those cats. I may want to be a hero, but I ain't dumb.

"What about the other Martians?" said McVitie.

We turned to look at them but, hey, guess what? They'd gone.

CHAPTER 11

IN SPACE NO ONE CAN HEAR YOU BARK

After the mass disappearance of the spooky bongo-playing Martian cats, we hopped back on the SEV and skedaddled back to the Pod. Gouger's new furry friend sat on his lap, purring away and grinning like a Cheshire cat.

Gouger was busy preparing to broadcast news of his discovery back to Mission Control, and was looking forward to getting a gold star or whatever it is Space Commanders get for discovering weird

Martian cats. But when he tried the connection, all he got was a blank screen full of static. It seemed that we were out here all alone. Gulp.

"It'll just have to wait till we get back to the Ark," said Gouger, cutting the switch on the communicator.

"Are you sure it's wise to take this — this, ah, *thing* back on the ship, Commander?" asked McVitie. "After all, we know nothing about it. It could be harmful. Shouldn't we check with Mission Control first?"

My point exactly. *Besides*, I added, *it looks like a cat*. That alone was reason for leaving Bongo Bill back on Mars. But no one was listening to me.

"Nonsense, McVitie," said Gouger. "Look at him. He's completely harmless. And Mission Control is out of contact. As commander of this flight, I am making an executive decision. Besides, this little guy is going to make us famous!"

The Martian opened one eye and looked coldly at me and Snowy.

"There's something fishy about that cat," said Snowy.

He was right. It was fishier than a barrelful of cod in an aquarium.

Back on the Ark, Johnson told Gouger that communication lines were still down between us and Mission Control.

"Odd," pondered Gouger, rubbing his massive chin. "Those communicators are state of the art, virtually indestructible."

And there had been something odd about the reaction of Tiddles to the new arrival. You'd think he'd have welcomed another kitty to the ship. In fact he had scooted off as soon as the Martian cat set paw on the Ark.

"So much for brotherly love," I said as Tiddles fled. Q sniggered and Tiddles looked at him as he passed. "Watch your back, rat," he hissed. "I might crave some alphabet soup one of these days."

We wrote Tiddles's temper off as jealousy. Gouger was making quite a fuss over the new cat, who was now occupying Tiddles's fave spot on the bridge of the Ark. I hadn't taken my eye off Bongo Bill since we'd left Mars, but after a few hours I relaxed a little. After all, I'd spent three weeks with one cat getting here, so I supposed I could stand another three with two cats. Especially since Gouger had made it crystal clear that if I so much as moved in the direction of the Martian I'd be back on Z-Block quicker than you could say "woof."

We settled down for the long trip back.

Nothing much happened for a while.

But a week into the trip Johnson disappeared.

One evening he was there kissing up to Gouger, as usual. The next morning at breakfast he was nowhere to be found. We searched the ship from top to bottom and turned up nothing. Zip. Gouger roamed around the ship, the alien cat in his arms, shouting for Johnson.

But he didn't show. In the end McVitie and Gouger concluded that he'd mistaken the air lock for the fridge and had been sucked out into space, a tragic accident. The air lock was where astronauts entered and left the ship and it was a very dangerous place indeed. Just being in there gave me the creeps.

"That fool must have gotten hungry in the night, half asleep, gone for a snack, got confused, pressed the 'Exit' button, and WHOOSH, out he went," said Gouger.

I wasn't so sure. Johnson might have been a creepoid, but he wasn't stupid. And only someone very stupid would "accidentally" get himself sucked out into space.

Johnson's disappearance shook everyone up, but we tried to settle back into the journey. I made a note to keep an even closer eye on our bongo-playing alien.

About ten days later everything went very pear-shaped indeed.

I had settled down for the night on a pile of space suits tucked behind the main engine compartment. I was asleep and dreaming happily when Snowy gently shook me awake by jumping up and down on my nose.

"About time," whispered Snowy. "Something's up."

The ship was dark and it took my eyes a moment to adjust. "What is it?" I asked.

"I can't find Q," said Snowy. "I woke up and he wasn't there. It's not like him to go off alone, not with two cats on board. I'm worried." His voice trembled and I could see the little guy was upset. Snowy jumped onto my back and we padded softly over to wake Dexter. We brought him up to speed and formed a plan to find Q.

The plan was that we'd have a look around. OK, it wasn't a great plan, but it was a start.

The Ark was a pretty big spaceship, and with air ducts, waste pipes, and electrical ducts all over the place, locating one small rat wasn't going to be easy.

We were in the corridor leading to the equipment repair room when I heard the sound of steps.

Someone was coming.

"Quick. In here," I whispered, dragging Dexter and Snowy into a small supply closet, which was now almost empty. We left the door open a crack and watched as Tiddles walked slowly past us into the repair room. We slipped out after him and tip-pawed over to the door. Tiddles stopped in the center of the room.

He had something in his mouth. It was Q.

He opened his jaws and let Q drop to the floor. He was dead. It looked like Tiddles had meant what he'd said.

"Quentin!" hissed Snowy, tears in his eyes. "I knew it! I'll kill that cat!"

I was about to do exactly that myself when something stopped me. Some sort of super-doggy sixth sense made me hush Snowy up.

Tiddles sniffed at Q and smiled. But just as he prepared to take a bite of the little rat a drop of sticky goo dropped onto Tiddles's head. He looked up at the dark ceiling and as he did his face crumpled in sheer terror. In the next instant a huge black shadow slammed to the floor, pinning Tiddles under it.

It was Bongo Bill.

Except he had swollen to the size of one of those large Martian cats we had seen in the cave. Oh, and he had sprouted a crop of slimy tentacles.

The Martian's burning, liquid-green eyes were the only bright thing in the room. One thing was for certain: I wasn't chasing *this* cat anywhere.

As we looked, the Martian's mouth opened wide, displaying a completely pant-wettingly awesome set of gnashers. It took one look at Tiddles and then, with a sound like jail doors closing, its jaws snapped shut with Tiddles inside. It happened so swiftly that Tiddles didn't even have time to scream.

The Martian swallowed and burped and then, for dessert, a long slimy tentacle shot out of the side of its head and scooped up Q into its gaping mouth.

"Bogus!" choked Dexter.

"Quiet!" I hissed. Too late. The Martian's green eyes swiveled towards the door and it sprang instantly after us. I slammed the door shut with a crash, trapping several of its tentacles. There was a howl of angry pain behind the hatch and the metal bulged as something heavy tried to punch its way through the steel.

"Run!" I shouted. Kind of unneccessary, really, because Dexter and Snowy were already legging it down the corridor. Behind me I heard the door give way.

"I told you, *never* trust a cat!" I yelled, hot-footing it down the corridor.

As we rounded the corner, Dexter leaped up to the ceiling and swung open a hatch leading to the air ducts. He swung from the opening by his feet, grabbed me and Snowy, and hauled us up, closing the hatch just as the Martian came around the corner.

We watched, terrified, through the mesh of the hatch cover as the creature padded along the corridor. It stopped right below us and looked up. None of us was breathing and I closed my eyes, ready for the end.

After a moment I heard an odd noise and I risked a peek. Below us something very strange was happening. The creature's tail seemed to be swelling. It got larger and began to vibrate. Then, with a series of popping noises, ten or more little balls of fur shot out and fell to the floor. The balls of fur lay still for a moment, then one by one they unrolled, revealing four legs, pointed ears, whiskers. Martian kittens! They were hopping up and down and making high-pitched beeping noises.

"Sheesh!" said Dexter. "Reinforcements!"

The new arrivals scattered in different directions, beeping wildly. They were looking for us. The big Martian cat set off towards the main control room where Gouger and McVitie were.

Except that McVitie wasn't there. He was right next to us in the air duct. I noticed him when I put my paw down on his nose. Ho ho, was I surprised! It didn't take more than a couple of minutes for the others to pry me off the roof of the duct.

McVitie lay trembling on his side, his knees tucked up somewhere around his chin and his thumb in his mouth. He was also coated from head to toe in a hard shiny plastic-looking goop. His eyes were goggling furiously, fixed on something that wasn't there.

"I think McVitie already knows about the Martian," said Snowy.

Next to McVitie was a pile of white bones.

"And I think we just found out what happened to Johnson," I said, looking at them. "This cat isn't joking around. Question is: When is it coming back to this little nest?"

We didn't hang around to find out. We couldn't get McVitie loose, so we just had to hope we could deal with Bongo Bill and his ten little helpers and get back to McVitie before he became the next bowl of cat food.

Checking carefully, Dexter eased the hatch cover off again and dropped down to the corridor floor, me and Snowy close behind.

The Ark was silent.

Dexter blew out a huge fart, shattering the silence. "Oops," he said. "Sorry, guys. Nervous."

"I suppose it could have been worse," I said, fanning the air. "Let's go."

CHAPTER 12

MAKING PLANS
FOR GOUGER

Bongo Bill had headed straight for the main control room.

"We have to stop him from getting Gouger," I hissed. "Otherwise we might never get back home!"

We kept an eye out for the smaller Martians. That's if they were still small. For all we knew, they could be the size of Texas by now.

As we neared the control room we could hear strange gurgling noises. It sounded like we might be

130 •

too late already. We slipped quietly inside. It was dark in the corners and that was where we stayed, out of sight.

Up front, bathed in a pool of light from the glow of the computer screens, was Bongo Bill. He was sitting in Gouger's seat with his back to us.

"Where's Gouger?" I whispered.

Just then the Martian swiveled in his seat and we got our answer. Gouger was sitting on the Martian's lap. He had an expression on his face like the one we'd just seen on Congressman McVitie's in the air duct. His eyes were fixed on some faraway point. "Not happening. Not happening. Not happening," he said. "Not happening."

But it was.

Bongo Bill was softly stroking the top of Gouger's head. We watched as a thin blue tentacle emerged from the top of his head and plugged itself into Gouger's left ear. Light pulsed along the tentacle straight into Gouger. There was a hum in the air and Gouger started to vibrate softly.

As we watched, his
ears slowly changed
shape, growing more
pointed.

His nose shrank, as did his
chin. Fine whiskers grew
from his cheeks and his
skin grew fur.

His whole body
became smaller and his
clothes slipped off
revealing paws where
hands and feet had been.

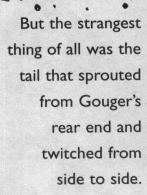

But the strangest
thing of all was the
tail that sprouted
from Gouger's
rear end and
twitched from
side to side.

He purred as the Martian stroked his head.

"Miaow," said Commander Gouger, looking lovingly at Bongo Bill.

There was no denying it. He had been transformed into a cat. And not just any cat. Gouger was now the spitting image of Tiddles.

"If I hadn't seen that with my own two eyes I wouldn't have believed it," whispered Snowy, his eyes boggling out of his head.

"I saw it and I've still got trouble with it," I said.

"It's all a plan, man!" said Dexter wisely. "I saw this on TV once when I was in a lab. I had to watch a lot of TV because, for some weird reason, they'd taped my eyes open. Anyway, one of the shows had exactly this happen. Alien dudes start replacing people and animals with copies. Then they, like, take over the world."

Me and Snowy looked at each other. If the monkey was right — and, let's face it, we didn't have any better ideas — we were all going to be turned into (YECH!) *cats*.

"We can't let that happen," I said feverishly. "Just think about it. You'll spend half your time stuck up a tree and the other half standing on a fence crying like a baby. What sort of life is that?"

"Well, it beats running on that stupid treadmill, old boy," said Snowy with feeling. "But I know what you mean. Still, I don't see what we can do. We'll be lucky to last an hour on this ship."

"I don't know, either," I said. "I just know we've got to do something and do it fast!"

I glanced at the computer clock. We had just eight hours before we landed back on Earth.

"One thing's for sure," whispered Snowy as she looked at Bongo Bill. "I'd like to wipe the smile off that pouncer's face if only for Q. He looks like the cat that's got the cream."

"That's it!" I almost shouted. "Cream!" The others looked at me like I had lost my marbles.

So I explained my cunning plan in detail . . .

Twenty minutes later we stood in the kitchen area of the Ark. It had been dangerous, playing hide-and-seek with the mini-aliens, who were prowling the ship. We ransacked the cooler and found what we were looking for: Tiddles's stash of cream. We grabbed as much of it as Dexter and me could carry, and we set out to get the next thing we needed.

In the supply room we grabbed a large plastic bucket and, armed with our finds, we snuck around the side of the Ark until we found what we were looking for.

The air lock.

The air lock was the most dangerous area on the ship — one wrong move and it was good night, campers.

The bare steel room had heavy doors at either end. One set, which we were standing in front of, led back into the ship. The other doors opened straight into space. This was where Johnson was supposed to have made his big mistake. Now we knew that his only mistake was being around when Bongo Bill wanted a midnight snack.

"OK, let's get this thing going," I said. "We haven't got much time."

Snowy stood on Dexter's shoulders and pressed a button on the wall. The big heavy doors slid apart and we entered the air lock, dragging the cream and the bucket. The door swished shut behind us.

We placed the bucket in the middle of the air lock and filled it with the thick cream. The rich odor floated through the room.

"I hope you're right about this, BD," said Snowy. "This has got to work."

We opened the air lock door and stepped quietly back into the corridor. We left the door open behind us. The bucket of cream sat in the middle of the floor. The trap was set. All we had to do now was spring it.

"Let's ring the dinner bell, boys," I said, nodding to Dexter and Snowy. The three of us were silent for a moment as we looked at one another nervously. Then we took a deep breath, opened our mouths, and barked, whooped, squeaked as loud as we could. The noise boomed out along the metal corridors and walls.

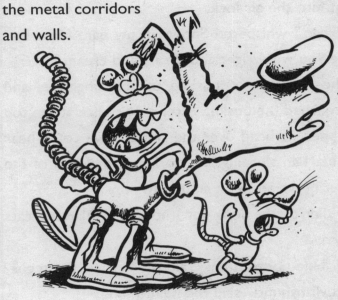

"That should do it," I said, a tad nervously, considering my doggy hero status.

"Let's get out of sight," said Snowy, glancing along the dark hall.

We slipped into a cramped storage closet and peered through the small window. A minute or two passed, and we thought we might have to shout again. Then we heard the first Martian padding along. It was a round, purple cat with a fat, blue tail. It looked cautiously up and down the corridor, then went into the air lock.

"Bingo," whispered Snowy in my ear. "Now let's hope you were right about cats and cream."

The Martian cat pushed up its sunglasses and approached the bucket. After a quick lick at the top it dipped its head over the rim and we could hear the Martian slurping like mad. In the gloom of the closet I gave Snowy a smug paws-up.

It didn't take long for the other Martian cats to arrive.

"Fribble doopshtum!" said the first on the scene.

"Luvlishypunt!" said the next in line.

Pretty soon they were pushing one another out of the way in their eagerness to get in on the cream.

So far so good, but it soon became obvious there was a gap in our cunning plan. There was no sign of Bongo Bill, the head honcho Martian. Without him the plan was a goner. And if he didn't turn up soon the cream would be gone.

I turned to see what Snowy thought but there was no sign of him. Dexter pointed down the hall. Snowy had slipped out and was heading for the Control Room.

"I'm going to give that big chap some encouragement," he whispered. "Wish me luck!"

"Snowy!" I hissed. "Wait!"

But he was off. The next few minutes seemed like hours.

Then we heard a roaring noise getting closer. Pelting down the corridor came Snowy, with Bongo Bill breathing right down his neck. He was not a pretty sight. The Martian had tentacles snaking out everywhere and his mouth dribbled stinky alien goop all over the floor.

Snowy got to the air lock doorway and raced in. None of the other cats looked up from the cream. Bongo Bill stopped in the doorway and slowly looked around.

"GRETFISHHHLER DRUPSNOTFILL TROMP!" he bellowed, and the mini-alien stopped drinking. They all looked at Bongo Bill, and then noticed Snowy.

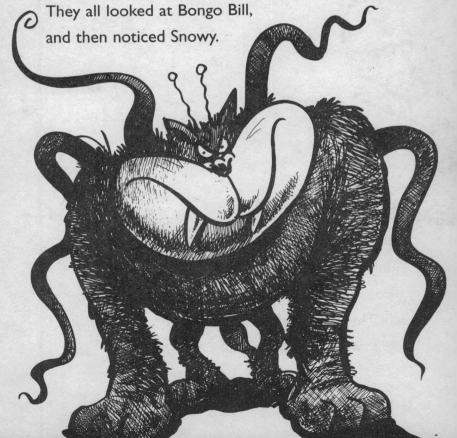

"Oh, no!" I whispered under my breath.

Before I had time to think about it I stepped out of the closet into the corridor. "Oi! Bongo Bill, or whatever your name is, you mega-ugly mutant," I shouted at the Martian. "Why don't you pick on someone your own size?"

I sounded a lot more confident than I was, but I didn't know what else I could do.

Bongo Bill looked at me and then at the other cats. Then he burst out laughing.

He was obviously terrified.

But as he laughed I spotted my chance and sprang forward, planting my front paws on his chest. Off balance, he staggered back and fell, rear-first, into the bucket of cream. Cream splashed everywhere. As the Martians began to lick the cream off themselves, Snowy and I made

a break for it.

"*NOW*, Dexter!" yelled Snowy, as we sprinted towards the door.

We shot forward as Dexter bounced from the closet and pressed the door button. As the huge steel doors started to close the Martians saw what was happening and sprang after us. Bongo Bill was almost free of the bucket.

I looked back and saw that we weren't going to make it. They were going to catch us. But in their hurry they had forgotten about the cream lying in puddles on the floor. Like a furry bunch of novice skaters they slipped and slithered on the cream, giving us just enough time. Taking a chance, I switched into surfer mode and, with Snowy clinging to my neck, I slid through them on a wave of cream as the doors snapped shut behind us. With an ear-splitting crash, Bongo Bill slammed into the door and snarled at us.

"The outer doors, Dex!" I shouted. "Do it!"

Dexter pressed the release button for the outer doors. "Elvis has left the building," he said, smiling.

With a soft hiss the outer doors slowly began to open. All the Martians turned to look.

Only Bongo Bill realized what was about to happen. He snapped his head back towards us and looked me straight in the eye through the toughened glass window set into the air lock door. He was doomed and he knew it.

As the outer air lock doors opened, it was like turning a huge vacuum cleaner on. In an instant the smaller Martians were sucked, screaming, out into the inky blackness. Bongo Bill clung to anything he could find, his tentacles grabbing like crazy at the walls. But there was nothing in the room to hold on to. He managed to wedge a tiny point of one tentacle into the edge of the door but it wasn't going to hold him for long.

I could see he was about to go.

"Hey, Snowy," I said, waving my paw at the alien cat monster. "Did you remember to put the cats out?"

And, with a final scream,
Bongo Bill was sucked into
space.

CHAPTER 13

I'M A CAT. I'M A CAT?

As the air lock doors closed we danced and whooped around the corridor. Our shouts bounced around the cat-free Ark.

"That was *intense*," said Dexter, chomping on a bag of banana chips. "I'd been saving these suckers for a big occasion. And you have to admit *that* was big."

I was high as a kite, dancing around with Snowy, when I felt the Ark shudder. The bumps got worse and the black sky we could see through the window started to turn red.

"Uh-oh, fellers," I said. "Let's buckle up. This might be rough."

We strapped in and prepared for a bumpy ride.

We got one.

All of us thought the same thing: Had we really come all the way from Mars, destroyed the evil aliens, and saved Earth just to be pulverized as the Ark plummeted uncontrollably into the Pacific? The Ark smashed through Earth's atmosphere into clear blue skies. We were going to get an answer soon. As we hurtled towards the ground, I was about to say a tearful good-bye to the guys when —

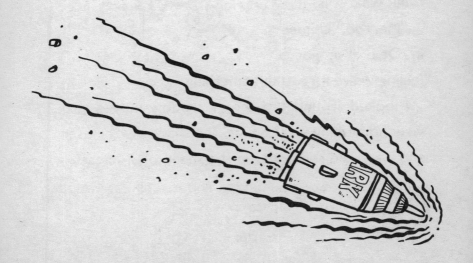

"Autopilot initiated," crackled an electronic voice, and we all breathed a sigh of relief.

Good old Autopilot guided us safely back to base, and I could soon see the familiar green-and-blue landscape of the training facility below us. We touched down smooth as a greased pig on an ice rink covered with butter.

"You know," said Snowy to me as the screaming engine wound down to silence. "There is one thing that's been troubling me, old boy, but I can't think what it is."

"Me, too," chimed in Dex. "I've got a feeling we've forgotten something."

I looked around. Just then a shadow moved into view. Something was coming. The shadow got closer and we could see it was in the shape of . . . a cat!

"We've missed one!" I yelped in a very embarrassing squeal.

The cat rounded the corner.

Tiddles! I mean, Gouger!

Of course. In all the excitement we had clean forgotten that Commander Gouger was now a drooling, goggle-eyed, bongo-playing, body-snatched, fully paid-up member of the Martian Cat Club!

He had a slightly rumpled look as though he had just woken up from a long sleep. There was nothing wrong with his temper, though.

"Get off my seat immediately!" shouted Gouger, looking at me. "I need to talk to Control."

"That's going to be difficult, Commander," I replied. "Unless you can find someone who speaks Cat."

From his expression it was clear that Gouger had no idea that he was now a pussycat. And a Martian pussycat to boot. "Good grief!" he exclaimed. "A talking dog! How long have you been able to talk?"

"As long as I can remember," I replied. "But this isn't getting us anywhere. Look," I said, pointing at a reflecting steel door.

Gouger turned to the door and looked at his reflection. Then, with a look of horror, he lifted a paw up to his eyes and inspected it. He swung back and looked at us.

"I'm a *cat*," he said.

Well, at least there was nothing wrong with his eyesight.

"A cat," he repeated.

"You got it, man," said Dexter. "Welcome to the animal kingdom."

"But . . . but . . . how . . . who . . . what?" he stuttered, before his eyes rolled back in his head and he passed out.

We all looked down at him. I was just about to say something when we heard another sound coming from the corridor.

"Now what?" said Snowy.

"This is getting ridiculous," I said.

Into the control room stepped Congressman McVitie. We had figured that he had gone the way of Tiddles and Q, but here he was, large as life. Bits of hardened alien cat goop dropped off him and shattered on the floor.

"He must have been shaken loose when the Ark was banging about," said Snowy.

"That's not all that's been shaken loose, judging by his face," I said.

McVitie still had a glazed expression on his face. A steady trickle of drool dripped from his mouth, which hung slightly open. He looked slowly around the room, spotted Gouger, and smiled. He stepped over and picked up the commander, and absent-mindedly began to stroke his head.

"Fribble shmip dabbly do do murffle qumsquachi," sang McVitie, bobbing his head up and down in time to his song.

His mind was fried.

As we stood around, looking at the frazzled congressman singing Martian jazz and stroking the furry head of the mission commander who was now an alien cat, the hatch to the Ark swung open and hot Florida sunshine poured in, closely followed by the Welcome Home Committee.

At the front was The Controller, her face flushed and excited. Behind her were a gaggle of white-coats and a group of soldiers. Mission Control had been out of radio contact with us since we had gone into the Martian cave. To say they were interested in what had happened would be an understatement.

"Welcome back, Congressman," said The Controller, holding out her hand.

McVitie looked at her hand then bent down and began to lick the back of it. "Shmurble burble furble durble," he said, smiling. The Controller whipped her hand away and wiped off McVitie's drool, a disgusted look on her face.

"Get me Gouger!" she snapped at the white-coats. "He's got to be somewhere on board. What a shambles."

In McVitie's arms, Gouger was mewing away like mad. "I'm Commander Gouger, Controller! I'm Commander Gouger!" he yelped. "I've been body-snatched, or transformed — or — *something* — by a large yellow Martian cat alien thing! I'm not a cat! I AM NOT A CAT!"

"Somebody stop that cat yowling," said The Controller to the soldiers. "Take him and McVitie over to the labs. We'll need to do some tests. It looks like they've totally cracked."

"Tests?" said Gouger. "*Tests?*"

Two of the white-coats grabbed him and carried him away. I noticed with some satisfaction that one of them was already unwrapping a thermometer and lifting Gouger's tail.

"Help me, Bad Dog!" he wailed. "Hellllppppp meeeeeeee!"

"Hey, Gouger," I said, smiling. "What goes around comes around."

CHAPTER 14

THE BIG COVER-UP

So we were the first animals on Mars — me, Dexter, and Snowy. We'd been up to the big red planet and come back without losing our marbles. Oh, and of course we managed to save Earth from evil bongo-playing Martian jazz-freak cat body-snatcher alien things on our way back. So we were heroes, right?

Wrong.

The Ark 2 was searched from top to bottom and,

of course, they found no sign of Gouger anywhere. They did find Johnson, or what was left of Johnson. They figured that McVitie had gone space crazy, offed Johnson, and left Gouger up on Mars. Only me and the guys knew the full story, but they didn't ask us — we were only a mangy dog, a loopy monkey, and an old lab rat, right?

McVitie was no use to them, either, since his noodle had been totally mushed by his contact with Bongo Bill. He just kept burbling away.

Gouger/Tiddles was undergoing tests.

Lots of tests.

And we heard from some of the gossipy guard dogs at the OSPEXA facility that they had turned up some *very* interesting stuff indeed.

Like the fact that "Tiddles" had blood that matched Commander Gouger's, and that "Tiddles" had human DNA (no, I don't know what DNA is either, but the dogs told us that The Controller went into full-scale panic mode after she found this out).

The tests also showed that "something" that did not exist on Earth was strolling around ole Gouger's system. With all this disturbing stuff floating around, OSPEXA did what any self-respecting spooky, sinister government agency would do, and hushed the whole thing up quieter than a nun with a sock in her mouth.

Gouger wound up in a high-security underground observation ward somewhere out in the Mojave Desert under twenty-four-hour guard. I suppose they wanted to see if he'd turn into some weird Gouger/alien mutant or something.

McVitie got the all-clear as far as alien blood stuff went, but as he wasn't capable of tying his own laces he ended up out in the Mojave Desert, too.

The rest of us were poked and prodded a bit, but when nothing interesting turned up, our services were no longer required.

Snowy was sent back to the lab he'd come from. "It's not too bad," he said. "Just lots of treadmills. At least I'll keep fit."

Dexter got a lucky break. Instead of going back to the testing lab, he got a cushy gig when he was snapped up by a movie company looking for monkeys. They were making a film about space apes ruling Earth, or some such guff. While they were making it Dex got to swan around in limos and eat as many bananas as he liked.

I gave him a few tips about the movie business; mostly along the lines of "don't chase cats and you'll be fine."

"Thanks, man. It's been real, dudes," he said. "What a trip!" And he was gone.

Which left me.

You've probably guessed where I ended up, right?

You got it. Right back in my old cell on Z-Block. Fester was delighted to see me. "This is becoming a regular thing, *loser*," he sneered. "I guess I was right about you being a Boomerang, hey, *Boomerang*? Haha."

I looked at him. He was his normal, burger-slurpin', one-step-up-from-amoeba, pimply, repulsive self.

I looked at my cell. My cell was still small, still damp, still gray. I smiled.

"Why you smilin', ya dumb dog?" said Fester. "What you got to smile about?"

I didn't answer him. I was too busy looking up at the night sky towards Mars. It lay there, a red ruby on a diamond-encrusted black velvet cushion.

And the fact that I was fifty million miles from that cat-infested wasteland of a planet was the most beautiful thing about it.

Mars?

You can keep it. I'm staying right here.

For the time being.